CLOUDWALKER

ROY HENRY VICKERS *and* ROBERT BUDD

Illustrated by ROY HENRY VICKERS

CLOUDWALKER

Harbour
PUBLISHING

Also by Roy Henry Vickers and Robert Budd

Raven Brings the Light (Harbour, 2013)

Harbour Publishing Co. Ltd.

P.O. Box 219, Madeira Park, BC, V0N 2H0

www.harbourpublishing.com

Design by Anna Comfort O'Keeffe

Printed and bound in China

Canada Council   Conseil des Arts
for the Arts   du Canada

BRITISH COLUMBIA
ARTS COUNCIL
An agency of the Province of British Columbia

Harbour Publishing acknowledges financial support from the Government of Canada through the Canada Book Fund and the Canada Council for the Arts, and from the Province of British Columbia through the BC Arts Council and the Book Publishing Tax Credit.

Cataloguing data available from Library and Archives Canada

ISBN 978-1-55017-619-3 (cloth)

ISBN 978-1-55017-621-6 (ebook)

The headwaters of the rivers that are born in this story are found in the land of the Tahltan Nation in northern British Columbia. This story is dedicated to the Tahltan people as well as the Skeena Watershed Conservation Coalition and all those who work so hard to preserve our precious rivers.

Northern British Columbia is very beautiful. There are three majestic rivers that flow down from the mountains, carving steep canyons and winding through the lovely flat lands all the way to the Pacific Ocean. These lands are home to many animals, plants and people.

In spring, the fields are covered in wildflowers and animals bring their young to the rivers to feed on tender new plants and enjoy the plentiful foods of this wilderness.

All life begins and ends with the rivers.

This is a story about three rivers. The people who live along one of these rivers call it *Ksien*. In the ancient language, *Ksien* means "the juice from the clouds." Sometimes it's snow; sometimes it's rain; sometimes it's fog, mist or sleet, but it's all the juice from the clouds. *Ksien*.

When Europeans arrived on the coast, they called the river Skeena. However, our people have been calling it *Ksien* for thousands of years. And we call people *Git*. So, the people along *Ksien* are called *Gitxsan*—People of the Skeena.

Long ago, in the days before there were any rivers, a young man lived among the people. It was so long ago that over the centuries, as this story was passed down, the meaning of his name was forgotten. Some storytellers call him Astace but we will call him Cloudwalker, and you'll soon know why.

Cloudwalker was the strongest of the men of his time. Every year the people had a contest to measure strength. Warriors had to pick up a rock in the shape of a huge ball. The boulder was big and hard to pick up. The winner of the contest was the one who walked the farthest while holding this rock. While most men could only stumble a few steps, Cloudwalker walked all the way from one side of the village to the other, and then walked back again.

Cloudwalker was the best hunter, especially with a bow and arrow. He also worked with a spear and a knife.

Spears were made by carving a wooden shaft and tying a sharp bone tip to the end. Knives were made with wood and a stone known as flint stone, which could be worked to a very fine edge. Most of the arrowheads were also made from this special stone.

When Cloudwalker was out hunting in the woods, he thought like a moose and he thought like a deer. This gift, and his generous nature, allowed him to provide food for his people.

Cloudwalker was also a good fisherman. He would provide fish for the whole community. Upon returning home with his catch, he followed the custom of making sure that the elderly were always first to be fed.

Cloudwalker was a great athlete, and he could swim underwater like a fish. It would surprise people to see how he could hold his breath and swim all the way across huge lakes.

But there was one thing Cloudwalker could not do. He could not find a special woman to be his wife. He wanted a partner who was strong like him, and who he could live with for the rest of his life. With no such woman, and no family, he spent a lot of time alone, fishing, hunting and providing for others.

Each spring, flocks of trumpeter swans stop to rest on the lakes in the north. They have a wingspan of ten feet and are the largest of all migrating birds.

An exciting idea came to Cloudwalker one day. He had a new plan to catch swans in a way no one had ever tried before. He thought to himself, "I'll be able to provide for all the people."

For weeks before the arrival of the swans, Cloudwalker went into the woods to prepare. He took the inner bark of the cedar tree and pounded it until it became very soft. Then he took the little strands of bark and kept twisting them together until they were very long. He did this until he had made a whole pile of string.

Soon the day came, and Cloudwalker watched the swans land on the lake. His plan was to dive into the water and swim underneath the swans. Then Cloudwalker was going to tie the strings around the swans' feet and pull them back to the beach.

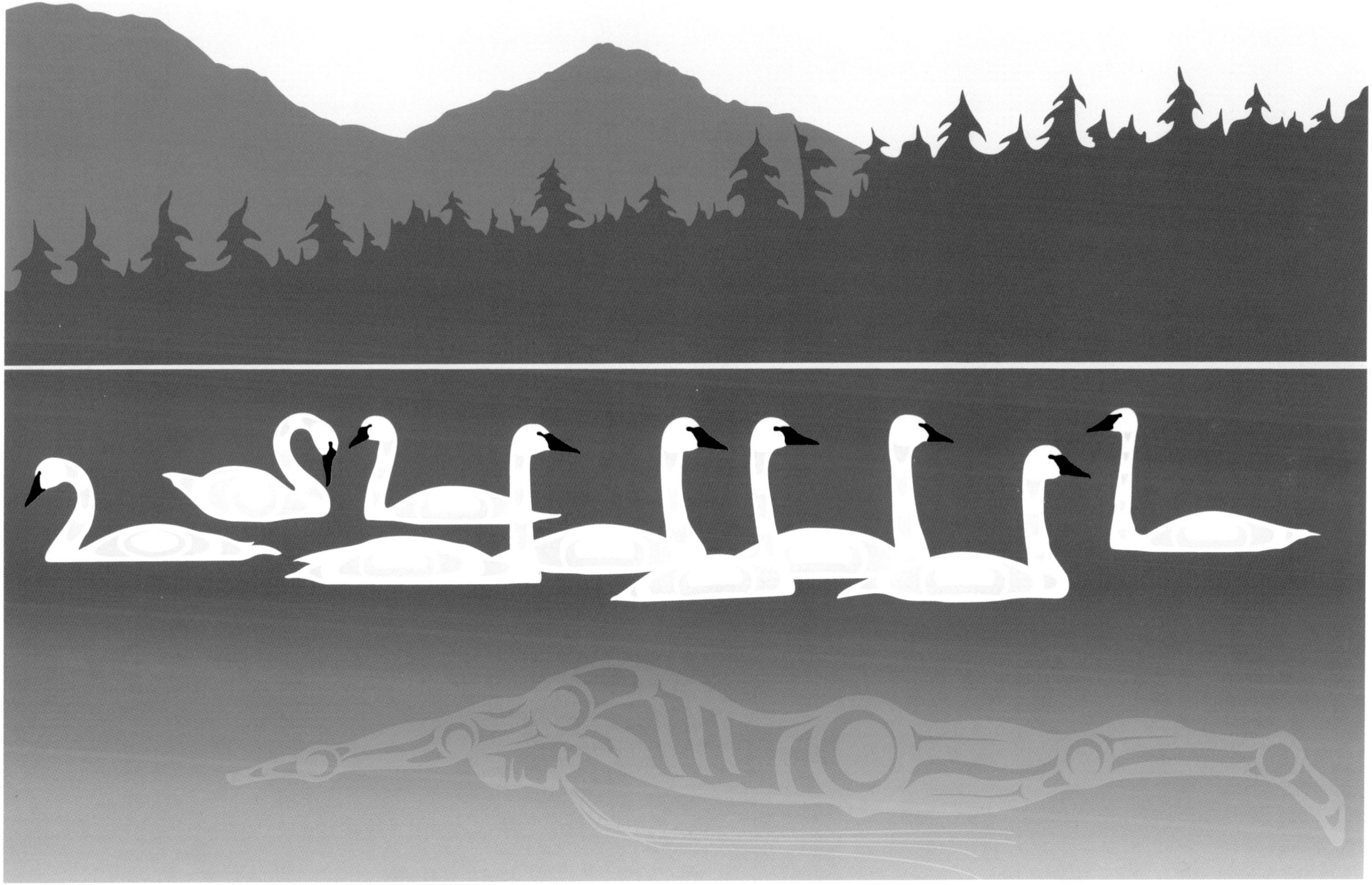

Holding the strings between his teeth, Cloudwalker dived into the water. As planned, he swam underneath the swans and quickly tied them up. But Cloudwalker got a little greedy and tied too many together. Once the swans felt what was happening to their feet, they panicked and started to fly.

The power of all the strong swans flapping their wings pulled Cloudwalker up and out of the water. Keeping together, the swans flew higher and higher...

Up.

Up.

Up.

Cloudwalker hung on and before long he was up above the lake, looking down. Pretty soon he was scared. He thought, "It's too far down. I can't let go now."

The swans flew over a rainbow and right up through the clouds. Finally the swans got tired of carrying him. They broke formation. Heading in different directions, the ropes pulled this way and that. Cloudwalker had to let go.

He began to fall…

Down.

Down.

Down.

He landed right on the top of the clouds. It was soft and welcoming, like a bed of feathers.

Catching his breath and calming down his heart, Cloudwalker sat and wondered, "Well, now what?"

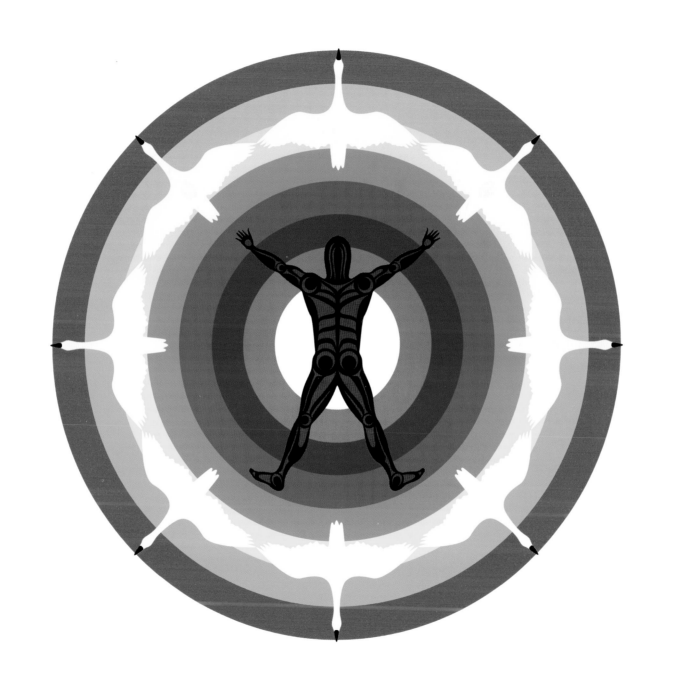

Cloudwalker looked around. There was nothing but cloud and sky. He started to walk.

Many hours passed as he wandered over the clouds. Then something in the distance caught his eye. He walked over to the spot and he found a *guloonich*, a waterproof cedar box that is used as a water bucket. The box was full of fresh water. It had a little hole drilled into the top with a long broken-off hollow bone from the leg of a tall bird, a giant blue heron. The bones of many birds are hollow which makes them light enough to fly. In a water box, they are used as straws.

Cloudwalker was tired and thirsty from walking for so long and took a big drink of water.

Thirsty as he was, Cloudwalker knew from his long hunting trips that he shouldn't drink all the water at once. He thought, "I'm going to need more water later. I don't know how far it is to get back home."

So he started walking again. But every once in a while, he would stumble, splashing a little bit of the water out of the box.

Up in the clouds, Cloudwalker could not walk in a straight line.

Now I'm going to tell you why.

Most people are either right-handed or left-handed and also right-footed or left-footed. If your right side is the one you use all the time, your right leg will be stronger than your left leg. If you try to walk in a straight line with no landmarks to keep you on track, you can't. Your stronger leg will push you harder and over time you will walk in a big curve. It will look like a crescent moon. If you walk long and far enough, it will turn into a circle.

That's what happened to Cloudwalker.

He thought he was walking in a straight line. But instead, he began to walk in a circle, getting even more tired. It was hard to walk on the clouds and every once in a while he would trip and fall down. And each time he fell, a lot of water spilled out of the box.

After he fell down for a third time, Cloudwalker lifted up his head and saw, way off in the distance, the top of a mountain coming through the clouds.

He was excited when he saw the mountaintop. He spent his whole life on the land, so he knew he could now find his way back home.

At long last, Cloudwalker made his way to the mountain poking through the clouds. As he walked down the mountainside, he thought he remembered the land, but some things were different.

There was a big stream running down the mountain. He had to jump over it to continue his journey.

There were lakes he had never seen before. Then he came to a mighty river. He thought, "That's strange! I don't know this river." But he crossed the river and on he went.

At last, he made it home.

When Cloudwalker returned, there was great celebration in the village. Everyone believed his story, because where he had splashed a little water, there were new lakes. Where he had fallen down, spilling lots of water, there were three new rivers. If you could fly like an eagle over the north country, you would see *Ksien*, the juice from the clouds. You would see the Nass River, the juice from the clouds, and you would see the Stikine River, the juice from the clouds. The headwaters of those rivers are in a semicircle at the three points where Cloudwalker fell.

That's how those rivers were born into this world.

When Cloudwalker made his journey down the mountain, he was the first to see a land blessed with the three rivers.

Salmon are born in the fresh waters of these rivers. They swim down through the eddies and over sharp rocks, through steep canyons and down waterfalls to make their way into the salt waters of the Pacific Ocean.

After living their lives in the ocean, the salmon make their way back to the fresh waters of the rivers. They jump over the same waterfalls that once carried them to the ocean. They scrape their way over the same rocks and they fight their way upstream to the place where they were born. Here they lay their eggs for future generations. New life will come from their hard work. They will die where life began.

After swimming thousands of miles, how do these salmon know how to get back to the exact spot where they were born? It is one of nature's precious miracles.

It is the rivers that are the life force for the salmon, and it was Cloudwalker who brought us the rivers.

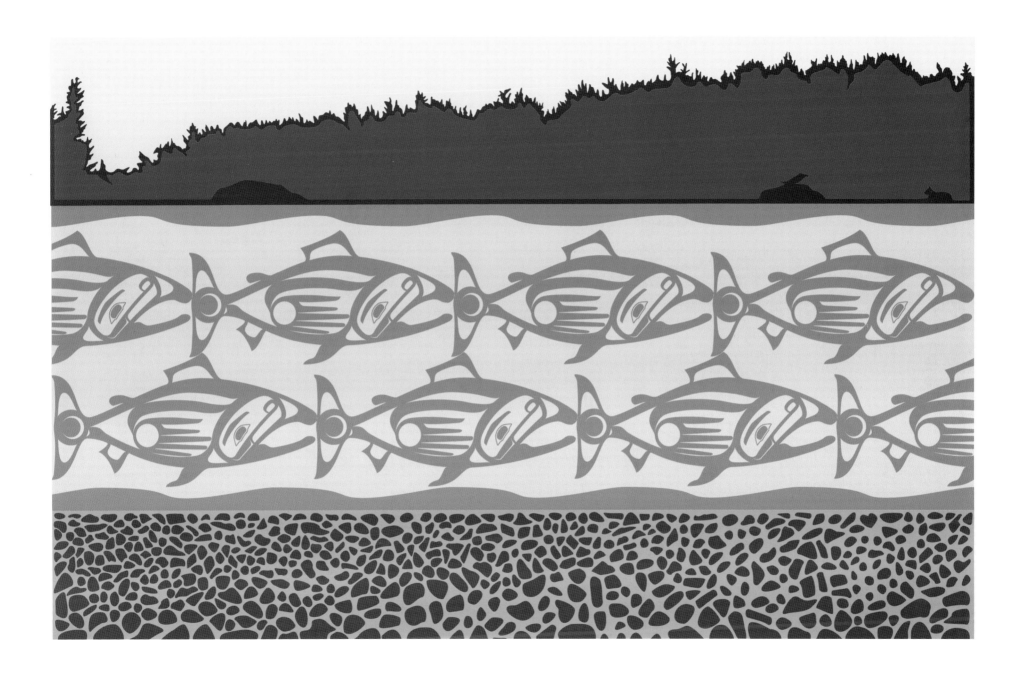

Every year, when the salmon come upstream, black bears and grizzly bears and the spirit bear (or white black bear) go to the rivers to feed.

The bears catch fresh salmon then walk into the forest, sit down and eat.

Bears are just like us, they have favourite parts of the fish that they like. Nothing is wasted because the parts they leave behind are eaten by the ravens and other smaller creatures that cannot catch fish themselves. And the parts that the animals leave behind aren't wasted either—when the salmon bones lie on the ground they decompose and feed the soil. This rich soil feeds the trees.

The salmon, the animals and the forests are all interconnected and the rivers run through them.

One of the last foods grizzly bears eat, after they have eaten their fill of berries and salmon, is marmot. They eat them just before they hibernate for the winter.

The greatest gift that one can give a chief on the Northwest Coast is the hide of a marmot. In the old days, after Cloudwalker came back from the clouds, we didn't have money. Instead we had beautiful priceless things like marmot hides. The marmot were only hunted by skilled and brave hunters like Cloudwalker and they were so rare that they were only given to chiefs. Some chiefs, when they got really old, had so many hides that they could have a marmot robe.

When a chief entered a big potlatch wearing one of these robes, people understood that they were in the presence of a very wealthy chief who had been to many potlatches.

The people of the Northwest Coast know that the richness of their culture and the wealth of the people comes from the rivers, the land and the sea. So, they teach their children to be respectful and responsible and take only what they need. They make sure the river is full of life to provide for future generations.

Author's Note

The first time I heard this story, I was a teenager living in Victoria. I used to visit the Royal BC Museum and one day I found a book called *Paddlewheels on the Frontier*. There was a tape that came with it. On it was a recording by Imbert Orchard of an old man telling the story of Astace. It was a short little story when I first heard it.

Today the story has grown much bigger as I have heard it from other people, and I have lived part of the story myself. I have heard it told that Astace, or Cloudwalker as I have called him in this book, stayed in the clouds a long time and that all the lakes and rivers in our province were the result of his falling down. I am thankful for museums and for those who realize the value of preserving the stories from the cultures of the people